Saint VALENTINE

Saint VALENTINE

retold and illustrated by

ROBERT SABUDA

ATHENEUM 1992 NEW YORK

MAXWELL MACMILLAN CANADA
TORONTO

Maxwell Macmillan International
NEW YORK OXFORD SINGAPORE SYDNEY

Atheneum
Macmillan Publishing Company
866 Third Avenue
New York, NY 10022

Maxwell Macmillan Canada, Inc.
1200 Eglinton Avenue East
Suite 200
Don Mills, Ontario M3C 3N1

Macmillan Publishing Company is part of the Maxwell Communication
Group of Companies.

First edition

Printed in Hong Kong by South China Printing Company (1988) Ltd.

10 9 8 7 6 5 4 3 2 1

The illustrations are mosaics created from marbleized and hand-painted
papers (adhered to gray speckletone paper). Printed on 100% acid-free paper.

Library of Congress Cataloging-in-Publication Data

Sabuda, Robert.
    Saint Valentine/written and illustrated by Robert Sabuda. — 1st ed.
        p.   cm.
    Summary: Recounts an incident in the life of Saint Valentine, a
physician who lived some 200 years after Christ, in which he treated
a small child for blindness.
    ISBN 0-689-31762-X
    1. Valentine, Saint—Legends—Juvenile Literature. 2. Christian
martyrs—Italy—Rome—Biography—Juvenile literature.
[1. Valentine, Saint. 2. Saints.] I. Title. II. Title: Saint
Valentine.
BR1720.V28S23   1992
270.1'092—dc20
    [B]   91-25012

In loving remembrance
of my grandmother,
Joyce E. Beach-Huebner,
1922–1987

In the ancient city of Rome there lived a humble and gentle man. His clothes were not as fine as the noblemen's, and his leather sandals were worn thin. He did not live in a grand house made of smooth marble, but in a small dwelling in a crowded part of the city. The man's friends and neighbors called him Valentine.

Valentine was a physician and practiced his trade in the tiny second room of his home. In that room stood a cabinet full of bowls and jars that held herbs and powders. There were glass and ceramic pots filled with animal fat and beeswax, and jugs of wine, milk, and honey that Valentine mixed with his medicines so they would not taste bitter.

When the ill or injured came to see Valentine, he would show them into the tiny room and examine them carefully. He cleaned wounds with wine and vinegar and bandaged them with fresh cloth. Or he might grind up herbs and roots in a small bowl to ease a visitor's pain.

When it came time for the patient to pay, Valentine would only accept what could be offered: a jug of wine, baked bread, or a new pair of sandals. If the patient had nothing, Valentine would say, "It was but a few herbs and prayer that have healed you, my friend," and send him on his way.

Prayer was an important part of Valentine's life too. But where most people in the city prayed to the many Roman gods, Valentine, and a small group of others, prayed to a single god. The Romans did not like these people, called Christians, who worshiped only one god. Whenever anything bad happened in the city, the Romans almost always blamed the Christians, even if they had nothing to do with it. Sometimes the Christians were put in prison or killed.

Knowing the danger of his beliefs, Valentine, who was a priest of the Christians, prayed for each of his patients, but only after nightfall.

One afternoon a man with a small child came to Valentine's door. The man worked as a jailer at the emperor's prison and had heard about the priest's healing powers. Valentine took the girl's hand and led her and her father into his examining room. The child seemed well, but when Valentine held up the oil lamp for a closer look, he realized why the father had come.

"She has been blind since birth," said the jailer. "Can you give her sight?"

Although he knew that blindness was one of the most difficult things to cure, Valentine vowed to do his best. From the cabinet he took down a precious copper box filled with a wet, waxy paste and dabbed a little into each corner of the child's eyes.

The jailer thanked Valentine and tried to pay, but the priest refused. "I cannot accept payment when it is doubtful the child will regain her sight. Bring her again next week and I will apply more ointment."

The jailer and his daughter thanked the priest and were gone.

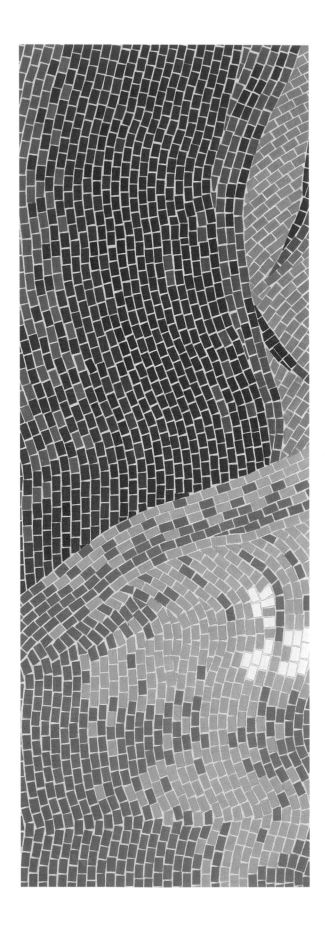

That night, like every night, Valentine prayed for his patients, but he prayed longest for the jailer and his child.

The father and daughter returned the following week and again the week after. Each time, Valentine applied a small amount of the waxy paste, but the child's eyes remained sightless.

After so many visits the three soon became good friends. Sometimes while the jailer stood guard at the prison, the priest took the child along with him while he gathered herbs and plants for his medicines. Together they walked outside the city gates and down the old stone road until they reached the countryside. In spring the fields were covered with bright golden crocuses, the first flowers to bloom in Rome after winter. While Valentine gathered white mandrake root for curing headaches, the child would gather bouquets of yellow and orange crocuses to give to her father when the priest brought her home.

Weeks went by until one day Valentine, who was expecting the knock of the jailer and his daughter at the door, heard instead the heavy pounding of Roman soldiers.

The soldiers burst in and began to destroy everything in the physician's home. They smashed to pieces the cabinet full of medicine. The precious copper box with the eye ointment spilled to the floor. Before he knew what had happened, Valentine was led to the emperor's prison and put in a dark, cold cell.

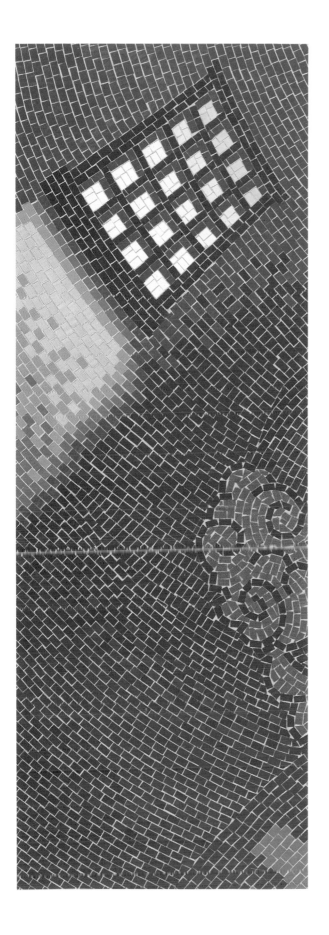

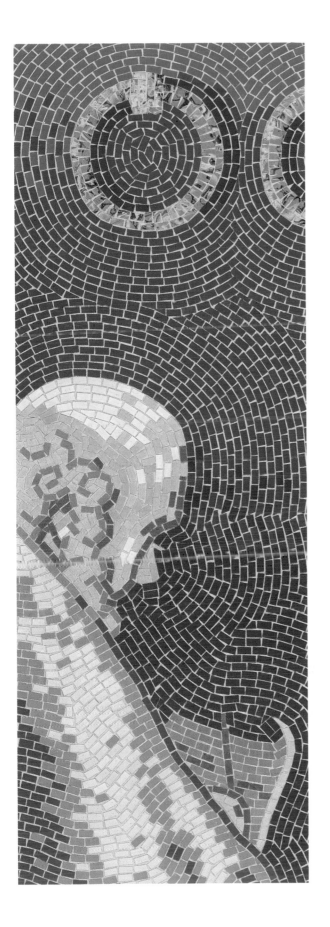

When the jailer heard of the priest's arrest, he hurried to the cell.

"There has been an uprising in the streets and the Christians are being blamed," he told Valentine. "Many have been imprisoned. The emperor has ordered it. There is nothing I can do."

Valentine slowly nodded and asked for a pen and ink and something to write on, which the jailer hurried to get. When he came back, the priest quickly wrote on the scrap of papyrus and handed it back to the jailer.

"Please give this to your child," he said, and grasped the man's hand in farewell.

Later two soldiers came to Valentine's cell and took the priest away as the jailer watched helplessly.

When the jailer returned home that day, he was greeted by his daughter. He slid the scrap of papyrus out of his waist belt, unrolled it, and handed it to the child.

"What does it say, Father?" asked the child as a yellow crocus fell from the small scroll into her hand.

"From your Valentine," her father read.

Slowly the child held up the blossom before her face and for the first time watched its color dazzle like the rays of the afternoon sun.

Notes on the text

Valentine was executed on A.D. February 14, 270, during one of the persecutions ordered by Emperor Claudius II Gothicus. Pope Julius I supposedly built a basilica (a Christian church with Roman features) over Valentine's grave. In A.D. 496 Pope Gelasius I named February 14 as Saint Valentine's Day.

However, the practice of sending love messages on February 14 does not originate solely from Valentine's note to the jailer's blind daughter (who it was said truly did regain her sight). The tradition is tied instead to the ancient Roman feast of Lupercalia, which took place on February 15. One of the customs on this occasion involved the writing of love messages by maidens. The messages were placed in a large urn and then drawn out by unmarried men who courted the girls whose messages they had picked. The two dates, February 14 and 15, came to signify one event: the celebration of love and Saint Valentine.

In France and England during medieval times, people also believed that at the start of the second week of the second month (February 14), the birds found partners and began to mate.

The crocus is the traditional flower of Saint Valentine.